The Fox and the Raccoon

The Hodja and the Soup

Loki Saves the Boy

THREE TRICKSTER TALES FROM AROUND THE WORLD

retold by Cynthia Swain and Brooke Harris

illustrated by George Banagis,
Dewayne Whiteside, and Steve Harpster

Table of Contents

TRICKSTER TALES

What is a trickster tale?

A trickster tale is a short story in which animals or other creatures talk, think, and act like people. One character, the trickster, uses clever pranks or traps to fool another character. Often the trickster is much smaller than the character he fools. Sometimes the trickster wants to help others, but other times the trickster only wants to help himself.

What is the purpose of a trickster tale?

A trickster tale shows human characteristics and problems in an entertaining way. A trickster tale often teaches a lesson. The tale shows what happens when people make bad choices—although some of the bad choices come from the tricksters themselves!

How do you read a trickster tale?

Pay attention to the title. The title will often tell you which character is the trickster. Each character stands for ways that humans behave. As you read, ask yourself, "What human quality, or trait, does each character represent?" Notice what happens to the main characters. Think about how the events in the story support the lesson that the tale tries to teach.

The main characters are usually animals.

The story is short and usually funny.

The trickster may have a flaw.

Features of a Trickster Tale

The trickster outwits another character to solve the problem.

The trickster has a problem or helps someone with a problem.

Who invented trickster tales?

Trickster tales originated all over the world, but African and Native American tales are among the most common today. The tales were originally passed down through oral storytelling. In modern times, many have been made into books and films. Some of today's popular cartoon characters are tricksters!

MEET SOME WORLD-FAMOUS TRICKSTERS

Trickster: Fox
Place: Japan
Background: Since people in ancient Japan lived among foxes, storytellers used this animal as a character in their tales. Soon, the fox became known as a trickster who could change into any number of other creatures, including humans. Like tricksters in other cultures, Fox could be either helpful or harmful.

Trickster: Hodja
Place: Turkey
Background: *Hodja* (HOH-juh) means "teacher" in Turkish. Hundreds of stories have been told about this wise and funny teacher who lived in Turkey in the thirteenth century. In many Hodja stories, people ask for his advice. In other stories, they test his wit or play jokes on him.

Trickster: Loki
Place: Scandinavia
Background: Loki (LOH-kee) is the child of giants. He has the ability to change into any animal. Loki started out as a harmless prankster who liked getting into everyone's business, but he grew into a liar, thief, and troublemaker over the years. However, as the tale in this book shows, Loki also used his powers to help people get out of trouble.

Tools Writers Use
Simile

Look at the word **simile** (SIH-muh-lee). Does it remind you of the word **similar**? Things that are similar are alike in some way. Most similes compare two things using the words **like** or **as**. Writers use similes to describe how the characters look and act. They also use similes to compare parts of the setting to familiar objects and animals. Similes help readers create pictures in their minds to better understand what they read.

The Fox and the Raccoon

One fine spring day, Fox met his friend Raccoon in a park. They liked to play tricks on each other. Both animals had a special power. They could **transform** themselves. In a second, they could change into any person, animal, or thing.

Each one could become a fish and swim to the depths of the ocean. Each one could turn into a bird and fly as high as a star.

"Raccoon," said Fox. "I think I'm the best trickster in all of Japan."

"Oh, no," Raccoon laughed. "I believe *I* am!"

"Then we must have a contest," answered Fox. "Let's begin right now."

"I can't," said Raccoon. "I must go to the statue of my favorite god, Jizo-sama. I wish to honor him with a prayer and a small gift. Afterward, we can begin."

Fox agreed to **postpone** the contest. He said he would wait a while. He even pointed out where the statue was before he left.

Raccoon took out a cloth as golden as the sun. He knelt down on the cloth. From a small pouch, he **selected** a piece of jade that was greener than the grass. He handled it carefully and placed it by the statue of Jizo-sama. Then Raccoon bowed his head in prayer.

When Raccoon looked up, the jade was gone! He looked around the statue and called out to see if anyone was there. No one answered. "How strange," thought Raccoon. "Maybe I forgot to place the gift!"

So Raccoon took out another piece of jade and put it at the statue's feet. He bowed and said his prayer. He looked up. Once again, the jade was missing. But this time, he was not fooled.

"Fox!" called Raccoon. "Show yourself. I know that you've turned yourself into the statue of Jizo-sama and taken my gifts."

In a flash, Fox appeared as himself. He smiled and said, "See how clever I am? I bet you can't top me."

"I will," vowed Raccoon. He thought for a second and then said, "Tomorrow, look for me on the side of the road. I will take the form of a great lord."

Fox laughed to himself. Raccoon was foolish to tell him what his trick would be.

The next day, Fox

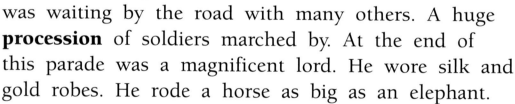

was waiting by the road with many others. A huge **procession** of soldiers marched by. At the end of this parade was a magnificent lord. He wore silk and gold robes. He rode a horse as big as an elephant.

"Bow down to the great lord," the soldiers commanded.

"Don't pay any attention to them," Fox called out to everyone. "That's no lord. That's just Raccoon. He's turned himself into a lord to trick us all."

The lord's face grew red with anger. His eyes burned like candles. He rode up to Fox. "Kneel before me, Fox. I am the lord of this land."

Fox laughed again. "Your trick did not work, Raccoon. Reveal yourself!"

"I tell you, I am not Raccoon!" the lord yelled. "Soldiers, **seize** this foolish fox. Put him in chains." The soldiers grabbed Fox.

That is when Raccoon came out of hiding from behind a tree. The great lord now laughed.

"What is going on here?" cried Fox. His face was as white as a ghost.

Raccoon had not turned himself into a great lord. He only tricked Fox into thinking that he had.

"Thank you, great lord, for your help," said Raccoon. "I guess that proves who the best trickster really is."

Reread the Trickster Tale

Analyze the Characters and Plot
- Who were the tricksters in the tale?
- Who did Fox fool? What did he do?
- Who did Raccoon fool? What did he do?
- Why did the tricksters fool each other? Which trick worked best?

Analyze the Tools Writers Use: Simile
Find examples of similes that use the word **as**. What did the author mean by making these comparisons?
- How high could the tricksters fly when they turned into birds? (page 6)
- How golden was the cloth Raccoon used? (page 7)
- How big was the lord's horse? (page 8)
- How white was Fox's face at the end? (page 9)

Focus on Words: Synonyms
Synonyms are words that have a similar meaning. For example, in this tale **think** and **believe** are synonyms. Synonyms can help you define unfamiliar words. Reread the tale to find synonyms for the following words.

Page	Word	Synonym	How do you know?
6	transform		
7	postpone		
7	selected		
8	procession		
9	seize		

The Hodja and the Soup

A poor man who had not eaten for two days went for a walk. He wanted to forget about his hunger. But his stomach would not let him forget. His stomach **gurgled** loudly. It made a noise like trumpets announcing the day. Then his nose got a **whiff** of something delicious. His nose smelled fresh soup cooking.

The poor man followed the smell down the street to the window of a restaurant. Inside, he saw a large pot of soup cooking over an open fire. To the hungry man, the soup looked like heaven on Earth. It smelled like pure joy. He stood there, eyes closed, breathing in the wonderful smell.

The restaurant owner came over to the poor man and asked what he was doing.

"I am enjoying the smell of your wonderful soup," he said.

Now, you would think that a restaurant owner would be glad to get a **compliment**. But this owner did not care that the poor man had said something nice about his cooking. Rather, he was quite angry.

"See here," said the restaurant owner. "You cannot stand at my window and enjoy the smell of my soup for free. I demand that you pay me!"

The poor man had no money. So the restaurant owner took him by his ear and dragged him inside.

"You must wash my dishes now as payment for smelling my soup."

Just then, Nasreddin Hodja, the wise teacher, came into the restaurant for his lunch. Hodja was known all over Turkey for his wisdom and fairness.

"What is the matter here?" he asked. The restaurant owner explained the **situation**. Hodja thought about the events for a little while. Then he said, "I will pay for this poor man."

"You will?" asked the poor man with a note of happiness. His eyes lit up like two shooting stars.

"Yes, I will, gladly," replied Hodja. He took three silver coins from his purse. "Will this be enough?" he asked the restaurant owner.

"That should cover it," said the restaurant owner.

Hodja then dropped each coin onto the table. *Plink, plink, plink,* went the coins. Then Hodja scooped up the coins and put them back in his purse.

"What do you mean by that?" asked the restaurant owner.

"That was payment for you," answered Hodja.

"Payment? That was just the sound of coins!" protested the restaurant owner.

"True. It is only fair that the *sound* of coins be payment for the *smell* of the soup," answered Hodja. "Now go back to your customers who are actually *eating* your food."

Hodja then invited the poor man to have lunch with him at another restaurant—one where the owner would not charge for the smell of the food.

Reread the Trickster Tale

Analyze the Characters and Plot
- Who were the characters in the tale?
- Which character was the trickster? How do you know?
- Who did the trickster try to fool? What did he do?
- Did the trick work? Why or why not?

Analyze the Tools Writers Use: Simile
Find examples of similes in the story that use the word **like**. What pictures do you see in your mind when you think of these similes ?
- when the poor man's stomach gurgles (page 12)
- what the soup looked and smelled like (page 13)
- how the poor man's eyes looked when Hodja offers to pay for him (page 14)

Focus on Words: Synonyms
The author uses many describing words and action verbs in this trickster tale. Some of these words are synonyms, or words with similar meanings. Reread the tale to find synonyms for the following words.

Page	Word	Synonym	How do you know?
12	gurgled		
12	whiff		
13	compliment		
13	situation		

Loki Saves the Boy

The authors introduce the main character. Loki is a kind giant who likes to help people. This is one of the traits of a trickster hero.

Most of the giants who lived in the North were as cold as metal. They were as mean as caged lions. Loki, though, was not like those giants. He liked to play tricks. But he often used his magic to help people in trouble.

One day, Loki went to visit a farmer. Loki heard the farmer and his wife crying.

"What's wrong?" Loki **demanded**. He asked them forcefully.

"Our hearts are broken," said the farmer. "A terrible giant wants to take away our son forever. He will be a slave in a mountain castle. There's nothing we can do to stop the giant."

"You must pray to Odin for help," Loki said. Odin was the king of the Norse gods. He often listened to the prayers of men and women.

"We did," the wife wailed. "The great Odin hid our son. He turned him into a seed of grain in a large wheat field. Despite this disguise, the giant found him. Odin saved him once, but there is nothing more that he can do."

"Then I will help you," **volunteered** Loki. He offered his aid even though he too feared the mean giant. "We will have to be smart about what we do."

Loki sat and thought. Then he asked the farmer if he knew the old boathouse by the river. The farmer knew it. Then Loki told him to put in a new front door and a new back door.

"Each new door must have a lock," Loki said.

The authors explain the problem that Loki faces. The reader begins to wonder, *Will he solve the problem? How?* To find out, the reader continues— eagerly!

The authors tell the reader that Loki is willing to help people, even if he is afraid. This shows that Loki is brave and has the qualities of a hero. Loki cannot beat the giant using force. Instead, he will have to use his brains. This is the way of the trickster.

"What good is that?" the **perplexed** farmer asked. He was confused. He did not understand how a boathouse could stop the giant.

The authors show Loki using the cleverness of a trickster to create a trap for the giant.

"Please do as I ask," said Loki. "Tomorrow, I'll take your son on a fishing trip. You'll see how I fool that giant!"

The farmer **doubted** Loki. He did not believe that the good giant's plan would work. Still, he put locks on each new door.

The authors develop the plot by showing Loki's plan in action. A simile creates a picture in the reader's mind of how well hidden the boy is. The reader is led to believe he will be safe from the giant—maybe.

The next day, Loki and the boy boarded a boat. They rowed out to the middle of a river to where the salmon lived. The fish had laid millions of small eggs in the water. The eggs were like grains of sand on a beach—a perfect hiding place.

Loki and the boy heard the giant running toward them. His huge legs made waves as tall as mountains. The boat rocked up and down.

Quickly, Loki said a few magical words. The boy was turned into a tiny fish egg in the water.

"Loki, what have you done with my slave?" shouted the mean giant. "You have no right to meddle in my affairs."

"Leave the boy alone," answered Loki.

The giant would not stop. He searched and searched among the fish eggs until he came close to where the boy was hidden.

Quickly, Loki used his magic to turn the egg back into the boy. The boy climbed back into the boat. They rowed to the river's edge. The giant stayed close behind, following like a shadow.

Loki told the boy to run through both doors of the boathouse. "Lock the back door when you leave," said Loki.

By comparing the giant to a shadow, the authors' simile helps the reader see how closely the giant trailed Loki and the boy. It adds to the suspense of the story, too. The authors want the reader to wonder, *Will the giant catch them?* **and then read on to find out.**

19

The authors build the plot to its climax, or main event. Loki, the trickster, outwits the "bad guy" and leads him into a trap.

A huge giant stuffed inside a boathouse is a funny ending. Remember that trickster tales are often funny.

The boy did as he was told. He ran through the house and locked the back door. The giant followed the boy into the house. Then Loki locked the front door. The giant was trapped! He is still there today.

Loki brought the boy home. The farmer **embraced** Loki for saving his son. The farmer's wife also hugged Loki, the good giant.

Analyze the Characters and Plot
• Who were the characters in the tale?
• Which character was the trickster? How do you know?
• Who did the trickster fool? What did he do?
• How did the trickster help the farmer's family?

Analyze the Tools Writers Use: Simile
Find examples of similes in the story. Explain what the authors mean when they . . .
• describe other giants. (page 16)
• describe the salmon's eggs. (page 18)
• describe the waves the giant made. (page 19)
• describe how the giant followed Loki and the boy. (page 19)

Focus on Words: Synonyms
Look for synonyms in the tale to help you understand each word below.

Page	Word	Synonym	How do you know?
17	demanded		
17	volunteered		
18	perplexed		
18	doubted		
20	embraced		

How does an author write a

TRICKSTER TALE?

Reread "Loki Saves the Boy" and think about what the authors did to write this tale. How did they develop the story? How can you, as a writer, develop your own trickster tale?

1. Decide on a Problem
Remember: A trickster tale solves a problem. In "Loki Saves the Boy," the authors wanted to show someone using cleverness to outsmart a bigger, stronger enemy.

2. Brainstorm Characters
Writers ask these questions:

- What kind of animal or creature is my trickster?

- What human traits does my trickster have?

- How does my trickster show that he or she is clever? What does he or she do, say, or think?

- What other characters will be important to my story? Which character will the trickster try to fool? Which characters will benefit from the trickster's acts?

Character	Traits	Actions Based on Traits
the giant	cruel; strong; determined	chased Loki and the boy, making waves as tall as mountains
Loki	clever; brave; magical	turned the boy into an egg to hide him; figured out a way to trap the giant

3. Brainstorm Setting and Plot

Writers ask these questions:

- Where does my trickster tale take place? How will I describe it?
- What is the problem, or situation?
- How does the main character's cleverness affect the events in the story?
- What events happen?
- How does the tale end?

Complete a graphic organizer like the one below.

Setting	long ago in the north
Problem of the Story	A terrible giant wants to take away a farmer's son.
Story Events	1. The god Odin tries to help the farmer but fails. 2. Loki tells the farmer to build a large boathouse with two locking doors. 3. Loki takes the boy out on a boat and hides him, but the giant nearly gets him.
Solution to the Problem	Loki and the boy row to the boathouse. The boy runs in and locks the back door when he leaves. The giant runs in and Loki locks the front door. The giant is trapped forever.

Glossary

compliment   (KAHM-pluh-ment) a flattering remark (page 13)

demanded   (dih-MAN-ded) asked for something in a strong manner (page 17)

doubted   (DOW-ted) did not believe (page 18)

embraced   (im-BRASED) hugged (page 20)

gurgled   (GER-guld) made a bubbling sound (page 12)

perplexed   (per-PLEKST) confused (page 18)

postpone   (post-PONE) to delay (page 7)

procession   (pruh-SEH-shun) a parade (page 8)

seize   (SEEZ) to capture (page 9)

selected   (suh-LEK-ted) chose (page 7)

situation   (sih-chuh-WAY-shun) circumstances (page 13)

transform   (trans-FORM) to change (page 6)

volunteered   (vah-lun-TEERD) offered one's services, usually without expecting compensation (page 17)

whiff   (WIF) scent or smell (page 12)